P9-DYB-873

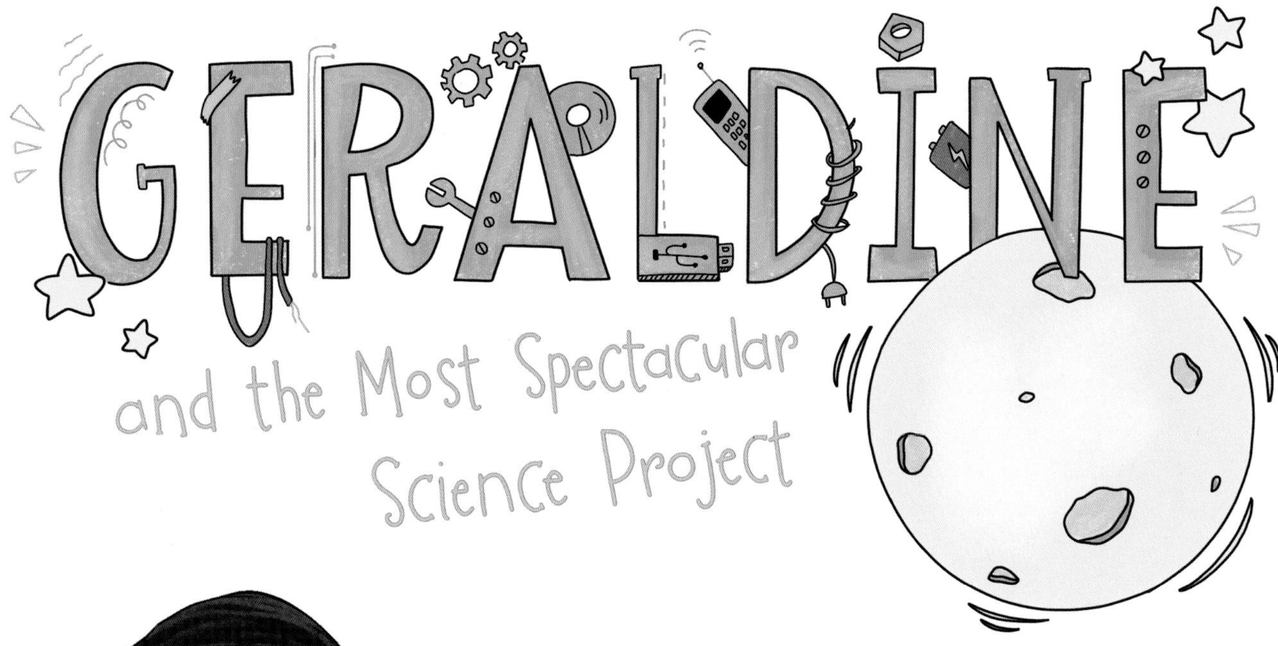

Sol Regwan
Illustrated by Denise Muzzio

4880 Lower Valley Road, Atglen, PA 19310

"I love being a troublemaker!" shouted Geraldine.
"Let's all go to lunch RIGHT now!"

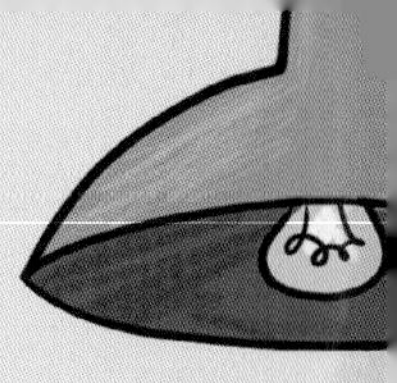

Yes, Geraldine was known as the loudest second-grader in Pinewood Elementary School. The teachers called her Feisty Geraldine. To the children, she was just plain silly—and often a bit mischievous.

Instead of paying attention in class, Geraldine spent the time daydreaming about becoming an astronaut. She thought about soaring through the sky in a rocket ship, floating and bobbing weightlessly in outer space.

She was totally fascinated by spaceships, stars, the galaxy, and, most of all—visiting Mars.

Geraldine had a wild imagination and loved creating unusual gadgets. She even took her mom's old toaster apart and added the pieces to her growing pile of old wires, screws, and assorted gizmos. Then she used the parts to build her own inventions. And fine creations they were!

Geraldine's favorite inventions were her portable tissue dispenser for cold and allergy sufferers

and her unique solution to wearing eyeglasses in the rain.

A
B
C

Unfortunately, her inventions greatly affected her mom's and dad's daily routines.

One day, Mrs. Hedley made an exciting announcement that really caught Geraldine's attention. "Class," she announced, "we are going to have a science contest. The winner will receive a first-place trophy and the title of Best Second-Grade Scientist!"

"What?" Geraldine thought as she looked up from the spaceship she was drawing on her math paper. "A science contest? Really? A science contest? This must be my lucky day!"

Geraldine listened carefully, which was quite unusual for her. Mrs. Hedley continued. "Every year we award a special trophy to the student who creates the most remarkable science project. Only one student will win first prize."

This was exactly what Geraldine had been waiting for: an opportunity to show her classmates and teacher that she was not just a troublemaker. "I can really do this!" thought Geraldine.

Screws
Tools
Wires
Gadgets

Right after school, Geraldine hurried home to begin her project. Her first challenge was figuring out what to build. She started by gathering her piles and piles of gadgets, screws, and electronic parts. She tried to envision the most spectacular science project—one that could win first prize.

She spent days measuring, cutting, fastening, and gluing her contraptions into various creations.

They were unusual. Some even worked. But nothing was remarkable. Nothing would win the contest—yet.

One evening Geraldine went out to her backyard, where she loved to lie in the grass, gaze at the stars, and look for her favorite planet—Mars. She made a wish on each star she saw. Her wishes were all the same. "I wish I could think of a remarkable project that would win first prize."

Suddenly, a brilliant idea popped into her head. "That's it!" she shouted, forming a circle with her right finger and thumb and looking through it with her right eye. "I am going to create telescopic eyeglasses that will make it possible to see Mars from Earth!"

Geraldine worked frantically for days.

She rummaged through her piles of gadgets and gizmos and found her father's old eyeglasses. She carefully removed the lenses from her mom's old camera. These would all be useful in bending the light as it reached the telescope.

Next, she placed the lenses on opposite sides of an old paper towel tube and reinforced it with heavy-duty tape. By placing a small mirror between the lenses, she completed both optical tubes. Finally, she strapped both tubes to her dad's glasses, using a strong glue she had found in his shed.

Geraldine sat back and admired her invention.
At last, her masterpiece was complete!
She ran outside to try it—and it worked!
She was sure she could see Mars!

The day of the science contest finally arrived. Geraldine and her classmates were busy displaying their projects.

Joshua revealed his erupting volcano, which spewed clay lava all over Mrs. Hedley's desk.

Timothy displayed his remote-controlled solar system that showed all the planets circling the sun.

Annie arranged her miniature ecosystem and explained how certain things affect the environment.

SCience
Contes

Then it was Geraldine's turn. As she walked to the front of the room, she heard her classmates whispering. One said, "She will never win!" Another said, "She is too silly!" Still another added, "All she does is daydream!"

Geraldine didn't care what they said.
She knew she was about to reveal something special. She stood in front of the class, proudly explaining her invention. The class became silent. Everyone stared, their eyes open wide. No one uttered a word. They had never seen such an amazing invention!

Then one at a time, Geraldine let each of her classmates, and even Mrs. Hedley, try the glasses. Geraldine had finally proven to the class that they were wrong about her. She wasn't just a mischievous daydreamer after all. She was a scientist!

Mrs. Hedley happily awarded Geraldine first place. "Geraldine," said Mrs. Hedley, "as winner of the science contest, you have now earned the title of Best Second-Grade Scientist. The trophy is yours."

Geraldine smiled as she gazed out the window at the beautiful blue sky. Thoughts of Mars came floating into her head. She was daydreaming once again. This time she could see herself defying gravity, soaring through space to become the first astronaut to ever land on Mars.

Look for the next book in the

series coming soon!

Copyright ©2020 by Sol Regwan
Illustrations copyright ©2020 by Denise Muzzio

Library of Congress Control Number: 2019946907

All rights reserved. No part of this work may be reproduced or used in any form or by any means–graphic, electronic, or mechanical, including photocopying or information storage and retrieval systems–without written permission from the publisher.

The scanning, uploading, and distribution of this book or any part thereof via the Internet or any other means without the permission of the publisher is illegal and punishable by law. Please purchase only authorized editions and do not participate in or encourage the electronic piracy of copyrighted materials.

"Schiffer Kids" logo is a trademark of Schiffer Publishing, Ltd.
Amelia logo is a trademark of Schiffer Publishing, Ltd.

Designed by Danielle D. Farmer
Cover design by Danielle D. Farmer
Type set in Hockey is Lif © Tom Murphy, courtesy of Divide by Zero Fonts § www.fonts.tom7.com / Cover font handdrawn by Denise Muzzio

ISBN: 978-0-7643-5898-2
Printed in China

Published by Schiffer Kids
An imprint of Schiffer Publishing, Ltd.
4880 Lower Valley Road
Atglen, PA 19310
Phone: (610) 593-1777; Fax: (610) 593-2002
E-mail: Info@schifferbooks.com
Web: www.schifferbooks.com

For our complete selection of fine books on this and related subjects, please visit our website at www.schifferbooks.com. You may also write for a free catalog.

Schiffer Publishing's titles are available at special discounts for bulk purchases for sales promotions or premiums. Special editions, including personalized covers, corporate imprints, and excerpts, can be created in large quantities for special needs. For more information, contact the publisher.

We are always looking for people to write books on new and related subjects. If you have an idea for a book, please contact us at proposals@schifferbooks.com.

Geraldine may ♥ science, but she also loves to read.
Catch up on some of her favorites from Schiffer Kids!

**I'm Going to Outer Space!**
Timothy Young
ISBN 978-0-7643-5385-7

**The 50 State Fossils:**
**A Guidebook for Aspiring Paleontologists**
Yinan Wang, Illustrations by Jane Levy
ISBN 978-0-7643-5557-8

**Bea's Bees**
Katherine Pryor
Illustrated by Ellie Peterson
ISBN 978-0-7643-5699-5

For my beautiful daughter, Olivia, whose spunkiness and curiousity inspires me every day.

–S.R.